D0535790

The One and Only Sparkella Makes a Plan

CHANNING TATUM

Illustrated by KIM BARNES

Feiwel and Friends
New York

A FEIWEL AND FRIENDS BOOK
An imprint of Macmillan Publishing Group, LLC
120 Broadway, New York, NY 10271 • mackids.com

Copyright © 2022 by Not So Tiny Dance Party, LLC. All rights reserved.

Our books may be purchased in bulk for promotional, educational, or business use.
Please contact your local bookseller or the Macmillan Corporate and Premium Sales Department
at (800) 221-7945 ext. 5442 or by email at MacmillanSpecialMarkets@macmillan.com.

Library of Congress Cataloging-in-Publication Data is available.

No turtles were harmed in the making of this book. Please do not bedazzle or otherwise decorate
any turtle's shell or place a turtle in an area where it may be in danger of falling from a height or
being crushed or stepped on.

First edition, 2022
Book design by Sharismar Rodriguez and Lisa Vega
Feiwel and Friends logo designed by Filomena Tuosto
Printed in China by RR Donnelley Asia Printing Solutions Ltd., Dongguan City, Guangdong Province

ISBN 978-1-250-75076-1 (hardcover)
10 9 8 7 6 5 4 3 2 1

To the biggest glittery poop that has ever lived
and my favorite world builder!
Let's keep building, Evie. I love you.
—C. T.

Today, I am having a sleepover with my new friend Tam. I am ready.

A glittery, glimmering outfit sure to impress? Check!

A collection of games to delight and inspire? Check!

A who's who of guests for what's sure to be the awesomest tea party ever? Check!

Actually, make that *almost* ready. The only thing missing is a castle fit for two royal highnesses.

And for that, I need Dad’s help. So I call to him:

"Dad!
Can you please come help me build a

castle fit for two royal highnesses?”

“A castle sounds like a very prime-time activity,” Dad says. “What do you have in mind?”

I show him the picture I drew.

Well, first of all, it's made of leopard stones.
There's a moat, and it's filled with red alligators!
And it's not just one floor, it's TWO!
The bottom floor is a candy shop, and the top floor is an art studio.
And this is the most important part—
there is a secret passageway that leads to a portal that takes you to Glimmeria.

I can tell from Dad's expression that he is very impressed with my vision for the castle.

The first thing to do when you're constructing a castle is gather all the materials.

But as it turns out, leopard stones are hard to find,

cardboard boxes are not sparkle-riffic,

and building supplies are not glittertastic.

Tam is going to arrive soon, so we get started on construction. I lay out one cardboard box for the first-floor candy shop and stack another on top for the second-floor art studio.

"Sparkella," Dad says, interrupting my progress. "Do you plan on using the second floor?"

I sigh. "Of course, Dad. It's the art studio. We have to go into the art studio if we're going to make art."

Dad nods, though I can tell from his expression that he has more to say.

I decide to show Dad that he has nothing to worry about, so I climb into the second floor, and . . .

crunnch!

At that moment, I need to take what my dad calls a breather.

I breathe in 1 - 2 - 3 - 4 and out *1 - 2 - 3 - 4.*

When I return, I take a look at the castle.
It looks *nothing* like I pictured.

And then I realize . . .

Dad looks around at our supplies. "Well, we could take some of these boxes and build a tunnel—"

"No!" I cry. "That's not how I pictured it. There needs to be a button. And when you push it, there are all these flashing lights, and then—*whoop!*—you're transported to Glimmeria!"

I'm sorry, honey. I'm not sure we have time to build that.

But I promised Tam we'd go to Glimmeria!

My castle is a total bust. No magic. No **SPARKLE**. No nothing.

I need more than a breather then; I need a walk.

A few minutes later, Dad joins me in the garage.
(He is good about giving me time when I need it.)

We made it SPARKLE.

Dad is right—his motorcycle used to be a mess, but we turned it into something really cool and special.

So, I think you have to take what you have and make it **SPARKLE** like only you can.

Take this tape, for example. What does tape look like in Glimmeria?

I think about it. Just because tape is boring and plain doesn't mean it has to stay boring and plain. I look around the garage, and the answer comes to me.

Actually, all of the answers come to me.

I race through the house gathering everything I need
to make my castle SPARKLE.

And then Dad and I get to work.

We lift and lower.

We build and bedazzle.

We paint and patch and polish.
And when we are done . . .

. . . it is even better than what I had imagined.

GLIMMERIA
Alligator Toy!
MOAT

Just then, the
doorbell rings:

Bing-bong!

I rush upstairs to
put on my glittery,
glimmering outfit
and wash up.

I give Dad a nod to let him know I'm ready.
He opens the door, and Tam and her grandma
are standing there.

"Sparkella, Princess of the Eleventeenth Realm of Glimmeria . . . your guest of honor has arrived," Dad says, just like we rehearsed.

Tam whispers in Dad's ear.

He gives her a wink and says,

And Sparkella,
may I present
Her Royal Coolness,
Tam, Queen of
Kittens.

“Your Royal Coolness, may I take your coat?” I ask.

“Why, yes,” Tam replies.

"May I offer you a refreshment?" I ask.

“May I escort you to our castle?” I ask.
I’m so excited to show it to her, I can
hardly breathe.

She nods, and when she sees the castle, her eyes go wide and her mouth drops open.

And I know that all of our
hard work was worth it.

SPARKELLA
GLIMMERIA
E

E